FRANKENSTEIN

Written by Mary Shelley

Retold by Beverley Birch

Illustrated by Rohan Eason

Collins

Chapter 1

I must write events down, at once, just as they happened. How strange they are!

We'd become trapped in the Arctic ice, in thick, blanketing fog, the ship dangerously hemmed in on every side, and little sea left to float in. Mountains of ice threatened to crush us or trap us here forever, to die of cold and starvation.

When the fog cleared, my fellow sailors groaned, and I, their captain, felt the same fear: as far as we could see, on every side, nothing but vast, rugged plains and peaks of ice, without end.

It was then that our anxious thoughts were pierced by the strangest and most unexpected of sights. A mile away – a dog-sledge speeding towards the north!

We took up our telescopes and could then see the figure in the sledge, guiding the dogs across the ice. It was shaped like a man. But it was a truly gigantic size.

How could anyone be here, travelling alone like that – hundreds of miles from any land, far out on the sea ice, this desert of eternal frost and unbearable cold?

We watched until we could no longer see him.

About two hours later, there was the roar of the sea
breaking on distant ice shores, the groaning of the ice.
We waited in fear. Just as night fell, the ice split and opened
a way for the ship to leave. Yet in the dark we couldn't risk
setting sail, for fear of colliding with treacherous loose,
floating masses of ice.

I tried to get a few hours of sleep, and at first light the next
morning, went up on deck. I found my crew leaning over the
rail, pleading with someone far below in the sea.

To my astonishment it was another dog-sledge, marooned
on a fragment of ice that had drifted to us during the night.
On the ice, only one dog was still alive, and a man, nearly
frozen to death, skeleton-thin from exhaustion and suffering.

In vain the sailors were trying to persuade him to come
aboard. Yet, he would do nothing till he knew where we were
going! Only when I revealed our aims, that we were on a
voyage of discovery towards the North Pole, was he satisfied.
Only then would this half-dead stranger agree to be rescued!

We started to carry him to the cabin, but in the sudden warmth he fell unconscious. We returned him to the deck and worked fast to bring warmth back into his body, rubbing his arms and legs hard. The moment he showed signs of life, we wrapped him in blankets and put him near the hot chimney of the kitchen stove.

Slowly he recovered. He sipped a little soup, and recovered a little more.

It was nearly two days, with constant care, before he could speak again. Watching him, I was often afraid that what had happened to him had driven him mad, so wildly did he look around, and so often did he plunge into moods of black despair.

So many questions we wanted to ask! We tried not to tire him, but on one occasion, we asked why he had come so far on the ice, alone. His face became darkly gloomy. His only answer was, "To find one who has fled from me."

We told him then, of the strange sight we had witnessed the day before.

At once he was frantic. He pressed us with question after question about every detail of our sighting, about the route the other sledge had taken to the north.

And he called its driver "the demon".

Days passed. Slowly, our visitor recovered enough to stay constantly on deck as we pushed further and further on between fields of ice. He fixed on watching for any glimpse of the mysterious sledge on that vast, terrifying yet magnificent whiteness.

I began to tell him of our goal to explore unknown regions, to find undiscovered lands, to know more about Earth than ever imagined ...

A shadow darkened his face.

"Do you share my madness?" he cried. "Hear me! You look for knowledge and wisdom, as I did once. Oh, my friend, I beg you – beware! Fulfilling your dream may be a snake to bite and destroy you, as it has destroyed everything and everyone for me ..."

And so he began his extraordinary and tragic story.

I write it here, as he told it to me, for you.

Chapter 2

You see, Captain Walton (he said), I had a dream like yours, once. I dreamt I'd use my scientific knowledge and skill to create an entirely new kind of being, one that would never, ever suffer illness.

I believed this journey of mine into unexplored science would bring great things to humankind.

I dreamt I'd become famous for the great gift I gave the world.

What I'll tell you now will fill you with horror and fear. You'll know of the terrible events that led me here, to this land of ice, searching for that demon you've seen.

My name is Victor Frankenstein. I was 17 years old when my ambition was born. I began my studies at the University of Ingolstadt. I was lucky – my teachers had great knowledge. They told me of the men who'd made the great scientific discoveries, who'd pushed human knowledge, peered into the hiding places of nature, and shown how it works.

Soon I was aflame with one thought, one idea, one purpose.

It was this: that others have done much, but *I* will do more.
I'll tread in the footsteps of those great discoverers, but I'll go
further, deeper – far deeper – into the unknown. I'll show the
world the deepest mysteries of creating life itself!

So I began. I learnt everything I could about the history of
chemistry and other branches of science. I became fascinated
by the new science of electricity, for as a boy I once witnessed
lightning strike an old oak tree. I stood awe-struck by the
power of such a force. At that time, a great scientist was
a guest in our house: he told me about the new theories of
electricity – its extraordinary, possibly unlimited power.

For two years at university, I did nothing but study these things. Often the stars disappeared in the light of dawn while I was still busy with my reading. I didn't make a single visit to my home in Geneva. Heart, mind and soul were bound to the wonders of science, to putting my feet firmly on the trail of the world-changing discoveries I planned to make.

For I'd begun to wrestle with the question, "Where does life come from?"

I'd realised that to understand life, you must first understand death.

So began my darkest researches. Days and nights in dismal burial places, looking at the dead. I was studying the passage of humans from life to death. I must know everything about the anatomy of the human body, and how it decays.

Night after night I haunted these joyless places, until in the midst of this darkness a blinding light broke into my mind. I discovered how life itself begins.

Even more – there came the day when I was able to make life, out of death.

I made dead, lifeless matter become alive again.

What an astonishing power was now in my hands!

I thought long and hard how to use that power. I never doubted my success. I'd create a being as complex as a human! To create a shell to receive this gift of life, one that had bones, fibres, muscles, veins, just as a human, would be difficult.

But I'd succeed. I didn't doubt it.

Many parts of the human body are tiny. Working with these would be slow. I decided therefore to create a being of gigantic size, about 8 feet tall. In that way, these smaller parts of its body would still be big enough for me to work quickly.

Now all I needed was the dead material to use in my experiments.

I went to graveyards, to mortuaries, to the dissecting rooms of hospitals. In secret, at night, I gathered the dead matter I'd need.

No one should know what I was doing – for they might stop me, and I couldn't stop.

Who can imagine the horrors of this awful, secret work! Remembering, my limbs tremble. Yet, my friend, you cannot imagine the feelings that blew me on, like a hurricane! I imagined a new species of being would bless me as its creator. I imagined many happy and excellent new lives would owe their existence to me.

If I could bring dead *matter* to life again, I'd even renew the lives of *people* who'd died.

I lost all idea of the outer world. I saw nothing of winter passing or the arrival of spring, the beautiful summer and autumn that followed.

I didn't eat, or sleep. I grew pale and thin. The ambition itself was enough to keep me alive. My dream consumed me. I'd become secretive, nothing else existed in the world for me, except this one task. My family wrote, begging me for news. I didn't write back. How could I explain? How could I spare the time to answer?

My success itself, when it came, would be explanation enough for them.

The leaves of the year had withered again before my task was at an end. Now, every day I could see success very close. I pushed on, and on, and on, towards my purpose.

But the days and nights of exhaustion spent in my terrible work began to make me ill. I burned with some kind of fever, became nervous, avoided people, turning away from them in guilt.

In a room at the top of the house, I made my laboratory for the final stage. Here, I'd conjure life – out of death.

Here, I'd create a completely new being, out of dead matter.

Imagine my state of mind, my dear Captain Walton, as I embarked on these final steps! What a journey to create a new and wonderful being, stronger, never suffering disease and weakness, happy and fortunate in its life!

At last I was ready; all was prepared. All now waited for that moment of life ...

Oh, my friend! If only I'd known ...

Chapter 3

It was a dreary night in November, rain pattering dismally against the panes. I collected the scientific instruments for giving life around me.

The lifeless thing I'd created lay at my feet.

Now to send the electric spark into it, and bring it alive.

It was one o'clock in the morning, my candle nearly burnt out, before the glimmer of its failing light showed me the dull yellow eyes of the creature open for the first time.

It breathed hard. A great jerk and shudder shook its vast limbs.

I stared in utter horror. With such care and patience I'd tried to create this being! Every part of him fitted his great size. I'd chosen his features in the hope they'd be beautiful.

Beautiful! His yellow skin barely covered the muscles and veins beneath. His hair was shiny black and flowing. His teeth were pearly white.

But all was only all the more horrible against his watery yellow eyes, his shrivelled skin, his straight black lips. An Egyptian mummy brought to life wouldn't be as hideous as that Thing. I'd gazed on him when he was unfinished, and he was ugly then. But when those muscles and joints were able to move, he became a Thing of Nightmares.

The beauty of the dream that had filled my life for two years vanished. Only shock and disgust tortured me. It was a grotesque, unnatural thing that lay before me. I couldn't look at it.

I fled from the laboratory to my bedroom. I paced up and down, up and down, unable to calm my mind. I threw myself on the bed, fully dressed, and tossed to and fro in the wildest dreams and most terrible nightmares.

I woke in a cold sweat, teeth chattering – and by the dim moonlight saw the miserable monster looming there. His eyes fixed on me. His jaws opened. He uttered harsh, meaningless sounds. A grin creased his wrinkled cheeks. He stretched a giant hand out to me.

I ran to the courtyard below, where I spent the rest of night, walking up and down, listening for the sound of the demon corpse that I'd miserably given life to.

They were terrible hours: sometimes my pulse beat like a drum; at others I sank to the ground in exhaustion. Horror mixed with bitter, painful disappointment.

At the first glimmering of dawn, I escaped into the streets through a grey, wet morning. On and on I hurried, not daring to look about me or return to my rooms.

At all costs I must avoid the dreadful Thing there, waiting.

It was in this state that my greatest friend, Henry Clerval, found me. It was such joy to see him, and so unexpected — I didn't know he was to become a student at Ingolstadt, too.

But my joy couldn't block out my terror that he'd see the creature and guess the reason for my bad health and my strange, fearful, excited mood.

I returned to my rooms with him, but ran ahead up the stairs to be first to my laboratory and stop him discovering.

My hand went to the lock. A cold shiver passed through me. That creature within! I threw open the door.

The room was empty. I stepped fearfully in.

Yes, empty. My bedroom, too, was empty.

My hideous guest had vanished.

I couldn't believe my luck! My enemy, the creature,
had indeed gone.

But I was exhausted. Now, disappointment and relief at
my friend's arrival came together. The wild state of my mind,
which I could no longer control, took over, and I fell down,
sick in mind, and lay senseless.

It was the beginning of a long illness. My dear friend Henry stayed with me for many months, nursing me slowly back to health.

Gradually, I could try to put the events of that terrible night, all the dark months of work before that, behind me. I couldn't bear the idea of more scientific work. Even the sight of the instruments was enough to make me ill again. Henry saw this, and removed every one from my laboratory.

Though still he didn't know what I'd done there. I never dared to tell him.

I saw now that my only chance for regaining full health was to go away from the university, to return home and take time to recover with my loving family. To forget. To wipe from my mind the monstrous creature I'd brought to life.

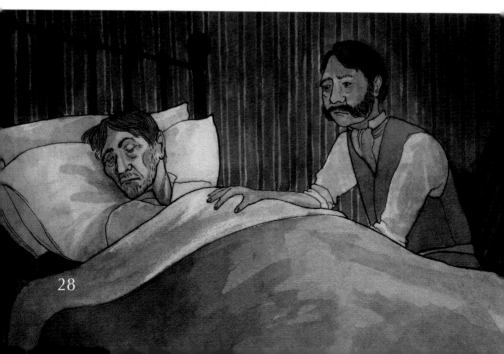

Chapter 4

On the long journey home, I tried to lose the idea I had of a threatening disaster that had gripped me ever since that night. But as I got closer to home, I knew I'd become the most miserable of human beings.

How right I was, Captain Walton! Yet, in all that I dreaded, I didn't imagine even a tiny part of the torment I'd suffer.

It was dark when I reached Geneva, the town gates already locked. I was forced to spend the night in a nearby village. In the night a fierce thunderstorm blew up, and I stood in wonder as lightning struck the peaks of the surrounding mountains, and seemed to turn the lake into a sheet of fire. Despite wind and rain, I went out and walked, all the time watching the storm around me, so beautiful, and so terrifying.

It was then I saw a figure come from behind a clump of trees. I gazed closely. A flash of lightning revealed its gigantic size and disgusting face. There, right before me, was the demon I'd created!

Another lightning flash revealed him already climbing onto the high rocks of a steep hill nearby. Quickly he reached the summit and disappeared.

Now my imagination was gripped with scenes of evil and despair. I'd given this creature life, superhuman strength and speed. I'd cast it out into the world. In an instant I knew without question that it was dangerous. It was too hideous to belong to the human race, and must be evil. I'd given it the will and the power to do great horror, great violence – I felt it in my bones. It *could*, no, it *would* kill and I must warn people of the terrible danger.

Yet even now I couldn't voice these thoughts. Who'd believe me? People would think I was mad. To claim I'd created this thing and given it life! No, these were the ravings of a madman ...

If only I could kill the demon, before he could harm others!

Even in the company of my loving family, I couldn't shake off these dark thoughts, or the guilt for my deeds. In desperation, I turned my steps towards the mountains nearby, searching for peace of mind in that beautiful, wild place I had known so well as a boy.

It was August and the weather was fine. I hired a mule, sure-footed on the steep, rough mountain paths. As I passed through deep valleys and rocky ravines, my mood became lighter. Huge peaks and glittering cliffs overhung me on every side. The river raged among rocks, waterfalls dashed down.

I climbed higher and higher. Now ruined castles hung among the mountains. Above it all, there were always the white pyramids and domes of the Alps, shining, and the eagle soaring above.

At last, everything seemed to gather round to try to bring me escape from thoughts of the demon.

It didn't last.

The next day rain poured in torrents and mists hid the mountains, and the black mood came on me again.

Again I fought it: I climbed to the summit of one of the mountains and a great glacier, dropping down to walk for hours across the sea of ice winding through the mountains. Surely this must bring me the peace I longed for.

It wasn't to be. I saw the figure of a man, at some distance, coming closer at superhuman speed. It bounded over the ice cracks that I'd crossed with such care and difficulty. As it drew closer, I saw that the figure was far, far bigger than a man.

Here again was the creature I'd created. I trembled with horror and rage. At least here, now, was my chance to kill him.

I prepared myself to fight him to the death.

He approached. The ugliness of his face was too horrible to look at. I saw the bitter misery in it.

But I saw the evil in it, too.

"Monster," I shouted, "do you dare approach me? Aren't you afraid I will trample you to dust?"

"I expected this greeting," he said. "All men hate the wretched. So I must be hated, and so miserable beyond all living things! And you, even you, my creator, reject me. You wish to kill me. How dare you play with life like this? Do your duty to me, and I'll do my duty to you and all humankind. If you'll agree to what I ask, I'll leave you in peace."

"I'll put out that spark of life I so carelessly gave you," I cried in my fear and anger, and sprang at him.

35

Easily, he stepped beyond my reach. "Hear me, before you pour that hatred on my head! Haven't I suffered enough? Don't pour more misery on me! Remember, you've made me stronger than you, taller than you, faster than you. But I won't fight you. I'm your creature. I'll be calm, and treat you as my creator, if you'll treat me fairly, and with kindness. You owe me this, for bringing me into this life. Everywhere I see happiness. Only *I* have no happiness. I was good and kind. Only unhappiness has made me rage. Make me happy, and I'll again be calm."

"Stop!" I roared. "I'll not hear you! There can be no conversation between you and me! We're enemies. Go far from me, or let's try our strength in a fight till one of us falls."

"Won't you look at me with kindness?" he begged. "That's all I ask! Believe me, I wish only to love and share life with humans. But here you see me alone, miserably alone. You, my creator, hate me — what hope is there for me with other humans? The mountains and glaciers and ice caves are my only home, the only one that humans don't try to take from me. These bleak skies are kinder to me than your fellow humans ever are. I beg you, my creator, hear my story. Then decide whether to put out the life you gave me. I beg you, listen: my tale is long and strange, yet it's within *your* power to change my miserable life and make me happy."

37

With this, he turned and moved away across the ice. I found myself following, my heart full. Curiosity and sympathy moved me. I turned his words round and round in my mind. I began to see that a creator does have a duty to a creature it brings to this life. He was right. Yes, indeed, I should make my creature happy before heaping hatred and blame for imagined wickedness on his head.

He led me to a warmer place, a hut, where we could talk. With a heavy heart, I pushed away my fears, and sat down by the fire he'd lit. As he began to speak, I tried not to look at his hideous face ...

Chapter 5

I can hardly remember my first moments of life (the creature said). All was faint and confused. I saw, felt, heard, smelt at the same time, though it was a long time before I could tell the difference between my senses.

I walked. Dark shapes blocked my way. Gradually I learnt to go round or climb over things. Light hurt me, so I wandered into the dark of a forest. Hunger and thirst took over and I tried some berries hanging nearby and drank from the brook. Then I lay down and fell asleep.

It was dark when I woke. I was cold and frightened and alone. Before leaving your rooms, I'd felt those first sensations of cold and covered myself with clothes I found, but these couldn't keep me from the damp dew.

I was a poor, helpless, miserable wretch. I knew nothing. Pain attacked me from all sides. I wept. At last I slept again.

A gentle light woke me. I saw a shining shape rise above the trees. It was the moon, I learnt later. It cheered me, and lighted my path as I searched for more berries. But I was still painfully cold. Then I found a huge cloak left under a tree and wrapped it round me.

Light, hunger, thirst, darkness, sounds, scents — all bombarded me. The only clear thing to me was the moon, and I fixed my eyes on her with joy.

Several nights and days passed. Slowly my senses became clearer. I found delight in sounds that came from the little winged animals. I began to see the edges of the treetops and the lighter sky above. I began to feel happier, and tried to make my own sounds to show this. However, the horrible noises that broke from my throat frightened me to silence again.

In time I saw the difference between the insects and the plants that grew from the ground. I found an abandoned fire, and delighted at the warmth I felt. In my excitement, I touched it, and burnt myself horribly.

I tried to keep that fire flaming, but when it died, I didn't know how to make another.

There were no berries left. I wrapped the cloak round
me and went into open fields to look for other things to eat.
My feet ached and blistered on the freezing, snow-covered
ground. I came across a hut. I was amazed that snow and rain
could not enter, and the ground inside was dry.

I went in. A man shrieked and fled past and across the
fields and away.

Starving as I was, I greedily ate the remains of
his breakfast, and was then so warm that I lay down
and fell asleep.

When I woke, sun shone across the snowy fields and I set
out to find more food. At sunset I arrived at a village, but only
shrieks of fear and stones and sticks greeted me. Bruised,
cut and afraid, I escaped to open country and hid in a hovel,
quite bare and so low that I could only just sit up inside.

This hovel was joined to a pleasant cottage, but after
everything that had happened that day, I dared not go into the
cottage. I lay down on the hovel's bare earth floor, which was
at least dry. And I was glad of it, for it kept the rain and snow,
and the cruelty of humans from me.

In the morning I made my shelter even safer from exploring
eyes, by covering cracks with wood and stones, and hiding the
low entrance to it. I spread straw on the floor. It was warm
from the cottage chimney, indeed a paradise compared to the
bleak forest, rain-dropping branches, lying on dank earth.

I could see the cottagers though chinks in the walls.
I watched a young man and a girl at their work in the yard
and the fields. And I was able to see into a small room,
where they sat with their father, who was blind and often
played sweet sounds on an instrument.

I saw how they were kind and gentle with each other. I saw that sometimes the young man made sounds and the others listened. Later, I learnt that he was reading aloud to them.

I was filled with curiosity about the lives of these people. I decided to stay, to learn more. After a while, I began to help secretly, collecting wood for their fire, leaving it close to the cottage, so that the young man didn't have to go far away with his tools to fetch some.

I saw how they told each other thoughts and feelings through sounds, that these sounds had a pattern that each understood, and that these could also be found in the books they read. I set myself to try to learn these patterns.

So the winter passed. I began to long to show myself to the family. But I knew I shouldn't, until I, too, could make sounds they'd understand.

I saw how fine and beautiful the girl and the young man were, and how graceful their father was with his silver hair. Yet when I first glimpsed my own face in a pool of water, it terrified me. I drew back in shock, not believing it was me. But when I knew that it was, the bitterest shame and disappointment overcame me.

But as the days lengthened and spring approached, I began to dream of how I'd show myself to these good people. I imagined their disgust at first, until, by my gentle behaviour and words, I'd win their friendship. These pictures cheered me. I worked harder to learn to speak, hopeful as spring changed to summer. I found a bag lost in the forest, containing clothes and some books. I was able to read them, and so I began to learn more about human beings, of what they knew of the world around them.

Something else happened. I'd discovered papers in the pocket of the clothes I'd taken from your laboratory. Now that I could read, I discovered your name, Frankenstein, for these papers were your diary of the months of my creation – all your researches, your experiments.

I felt sick as I read.

I began to hate you, for creating a monster so hideous that even you turned from me.

I plunged into the deepest misery. Yet when I thought of my cottagers, hope sprang up again. Could they, gentle and loving as they were, turn away someone who wanted only their friendship? But I was afraid I'd fail, and knew I must prepare carefully.

I held on to my hope, even though it often vanished when I saw my reflection in the water or my shadow on the ground. Autumn came and went, and then winter. A full turn of the seasons had passed since I became alive.

There came the day when the young people went for a walk, leaving their father alone, playing his musical instrument. My heart beat fast, but I knocked. The old man called a welcome. I went in. We sat talking, for he with his blindness couldn't see me and only heard my words. He was kind and interested. I felt braver, and began to reveal my story to him.

Outside, I heard the step of the returning young people. They came in. At sight of me, the girl fainted. The young man darted forward and tore me from his father, dashed me to the ground and struck me violently with a stick.

I could have ripped him limb from limb, as a lion can kill an antelope. But my heart just sank in bitter disappointment, and I held back my anger. In pain and misery, I left the cottage and in the general uproar, I escaped unseen into my hovel.

When night fell and I'd no longer be seen, I left the hovel, and wandered in the wood, howling my misery. Cold stars shone down, teasing me. Trees waved bare branches above me. From that moment, I felt only hatred for humans, and for you who'd brought me into this cruel world to suffer such loneliness.

Through the next day I hid in the forest, and when night fell, crawled into my hovel to await the moment when the family woke. I'd begun to hope again. Perhaps I'd approached them carelessly. Perhaps they needed time to get used to me ...

False hope! The family had left. They never returned. My only link to the world of humans was broken.

Despair turned to fury. I allowed myself to be carried on a wave of revenge and hatred.

I burnt the cottage to the ground and left, to fly far from humans and their harshness and cruelty to me. My thoughts turned to you. From you I'd demand help. And from your papers I learnt where to find you.

My travels were long, and my suffering great. I travelled only at night, fearful of meeting humans. The closer I came to where you lived, the stronger my desire for revenge.

Yet again, as spring came nearer, and the air warmed with early sunshine, I dared to forget my loneliness and ugliness. One day I was almost happy, and stepped out from the trees to look at the beautiful scene around me. At that moment a young girl came running along the river. Suddenly she slipped and fell in, and was swept into the deep stream. I rushed into the water, and with a fierce struggle against the strong current, I dragged her to the bank. She lay still, and I tried to bring her back to consciousness, finally succeeded, but as she opened her eyes, a man ran out of the wood, tore her from me and ran away among the trees, carrying her. I sped after him, I hardly know why, but he aimed a gun and fired. I fell to the ground, twisting with the pain of shattered flesh and bone.

This was the reward for saving the girl's life! The gentleness I felt only moments before gave way to rage and gnashing of teeth. Made worse by my agonising wound, I vowed eternal hatred and vengeance on all humans.

I hid in the forest, trying to recover from the wound, before I was able to travel on to Geneva, and to you, my creator. For some time I haunted the places near you. Sometimes I almost approached you. Sometimes I decided to go far way, forever.

At last I wandered towards these mountains and have travelled their immense ranges, more and more burning with a wish that only you can grant.

We won't part until you've promised to grant it.
I'm alone, and miserable. Humans won't be friends with me. But someone made as I am, rejected by humans in the same way I am rejected – such a being will want to be my friend.

You can create this being. You *must* create it.

You must make a friend for me.

Chapter 6

The creature finished, and watched me. His tale had made me feel sorry for him, but I could think only of his huge size. What harm he could do with such power! I said nothing.

He became so upset, his face twisting and his eyes flashing in a way too horrible to look at. "You can't refuse me!" he roared. "I'm hated by everyone. Everyone runs from me. Give me a companion, who'll be like me, and share my life! Don't deny me!"

I was moved. I shuddered at the thought of what harm could be done by two creatures with such power, but I saw, too, that he was right. I, his maker, owed him whatever happiness I had the power to give him.

He saw my changing face and went on quickly, "If you agree, you won't see us again. Nor will any other human ever see us; we'll go to the wildest parts of the world, where humans never go."

His words had a strong effect on me. But I'd avoided looking at him: when I did, I saw this ugly mass that moved and talked and my heart sickened again. I tried to push these feelings away, and told myself that I indeed had no right to keep from him any happiness I could give.

"I agree," I said finally, "if you swear that you'll go far away as soon as I deliver a friend of your same kind, to go with you."

"I swear," he cried, "by the sun, and by the blue sky, and by the fire of love that burns in my heart, that if you grant my wish, you'll never see me again. Start your work. I'll watch every moment of your progress, and then I'll go."

With these words, he suddenly left, fearful perhaps that I'd change my mind. I watched him go down the mountain faster than an eagle flies, to vanish amongst the ragged ice-shapes.

As I returned home, my heart was heavy, and my step slow. I struggled with wild thoughts. Such dangers in creating yet another being like him!

But I had to do it. Deep down, I feared the revenge of the disappointed monster if I didn't.

There had been some new, important scientific work in England, and I thought it might help me to talk to these men of science before I created the new being.

I didn't tell my family this true reason, but said the journey was to get fully well again, and they agreed.

My dear friend Henry quickly offered to come with me. We set off, passing through Germany and Holland, then crossing the sea to England's shores. Over the months that followed, we explored England together, and for a time I put off my task, and lost myself in new sights and in Henry's happy and interesting company.

But at the back of my mind, I feared the creature's disappointment. I couldn't delay any longer. If I did, he might go to Geneva and take revenge on my family.

This idea tormented me. I could no longer lose myself in exploring new places, and must turn to the task.

I lied to Henry. I said that I wished to spend time travelling alone, and thinking, and though he was worried for me, he agreed, and we parted.

I fixed on a remote place in the Orkney islands as the scene of my work. The island was hardly more than a bare rock. Waves beat it on all sides. Few people lived there. A few cows grazed on scraggy pasture. Vegetable and bread, and even fresh water had to be fetched from the mainland, five miles away. But I'd no doubt the monster would find me, that he was close.

I rented a hut — a miserable, poor two rooms, but with a bed and a few sticks of furniture in one room, and my equipment moved in to the other, I was ready.

I worked steadily. Yet every hour, every day, the task became more horrible, and I more fearful of what I was doing. What dangers I was giving my fellow humans, by bringing into their world yet another being of such enormous power, such brain, such feeling! The first time, excitement had blinded me to the horrors of the work. Now horror was with me every moment. As I got closer, and the new creature was nearly ready to receive life, I became filled by a sense of doom ahead.

The creature believed that a companion of the same kind would be a friend. But they might find each other revolting. Rage and disappointment might overtake them. Revenge might fill both hearts!

My promise to create another was wicked. As I stood there, thinking, I looked up at the window. There was the demon, looking in. I saw a grin spread across his terrible face, as he gazed at the new creature on the table.

I grabbed the thing and tore it to pieces.

A howl of despair came from him, a scream of anger and revenge and pain. He disappeared from view.

Hours passed. I stared out at the sea, but everything was quiet. Only fishermen were out on the water now and their voices carried on the breeze.

Then I heard the paddle of oars, and someone landing near my hut, and footsteps nearing.

There stood the demon again.

"I won't do what you ask," I said.

"Remember, I have power," he cried. "I can make you so miserable that the light of day will be hateful. You're my creator, but I'm your master. Obey me!"

"I won't!" I repeated.

"Beware!" he roared. "You can blast other feelings from me, but not revenge! Beware, for I'm fearless and therefore more powerful ... " and he rushed away, shrieking. I saw him in his boat, which shot across the water like an arrow and was soon lost among the waves.

His words rang in my ears. In torment I walked up and down my room. I should have followed him, fought him, stopped him from doing harm ever again.

But I hadn't, and he'd reach the mainland ...

Dawn came. In great distress I wandered about my rock. Dusk fell again, and a fishing boat brought a letter from Henry to tell me that he must return home soon, begging me to join him in Scotland so that we could travel back to England together.

His letter gave me new energy. I decided to leave immediately.

There was just one task to perform first.

Chapter 7

I must go to the room where I'd worked and handle things that made me sick to look at them.

I unlocked the door. The remains of the half-finished creature I'd destroyed lay scattered on the floor. I almost felt as if I'd destroyed a living human being.

I collected the pieces and packed them in a basket, and put heavy stones on top. As the moon rose, I took a little sailing boat and went out to deep water, waiting till a cloud hid the moon and gave a moment of darkness. I tipped the basket over the side, and heard it gurgle to the bottom of the ocean, carrying its dreadful cargo.

The task done, my heart was lighter, and a breeze seemed to blow away some of my heavy gloom. I sailed on a little, and then fixed the rudder to hold the same course. I lay down in the boat to enjoy the night, the wide sea, the great sky, the music of the water trickling past. Everything calmed me, and I slept.

When I woke, it was already day, and brisk winds had driven me far, far from my island. I tried to change course, but rolling waves threatened to swamp me. I'd a burning thirst. Visions of starvation, of drowning filled my head.

Hours passed before the wind and the sea calmed, and I saw a line of land on the horizon. I was able to sail towards it, and in time reached a little town and a neat harbour, and landed with joy at my escape. People gathered swiftly round me.

But to my astonishment they greeted me with rough words and arrested me. They told of a murder that had taken place, and accused me of being the killer.

I protested, but was taken to see the body in its coffin.

My dear friend Henry, lifeless. The marks of giant fingers were black on his throat.

My mind and body couldn't take my agony. I was carried from the room in a fit. Fever followed, and I descended into madness. I screamed for help to kill the monster. I felt his fingers at my own neck. I saw again and again my dearest friend, so generous to me, now victim to the revenge of the monster I'd made, the enemy I'd let loose among the people I cared for. Friends, family, all now facing his terrible revenge.

For three months I hung on the point of death in that prison.

I recovered, slowly. Lawyers proved that I was far away in the Orkneys when Henry's body was found, and couldn't be his killer.

Freed from prison, I vowed to spend the rest of my life tracking that monster. I'd pursue him to the ends of the earth, into the furthest reaches of the wilds. I'd find him, and I'd destroy him.

There was nothing else for me. I'd devote myself, in life or death, to his destruction.

Chapter 8

So began my wanderings. They'll stop only when my life stops. I've crossed vast parts of the earth. I've experienced deserts and wilderness, climbed mountains, swum rivers, sailed the oceans.

Thoughts of revenge drove me on, and kept me alive.

At times I heard his laugh ring loud, and knew he was near. At times he left me clues and drew me on.

His trail led me north, into the lands of snow and ice.

I bought a sledge and dogs, and crossed the snows with unimaginable speed. By the time I reached the edge of the vast Arctic ocean, I had news: a giant of a man was a day's travel ahead; he had a sledge and dogs and had set out across the sea ice in a direction that led to no land; he'd surely perish there, crushed by breaking ice or frozen to death.

I exchanged my land sledge for another that could cross the mountains of sea ice, and I left the land.

For weeks I pursued him. My dogs struggled bravely
up the sea-ice mountains, and one died. Then I nearly
despaired, viewing the huge expanse ahead of me, unchanging
and threatening.

But then my eye caught the dark speck moving across the
ice with incredible speed.

Hope was in my heart again, and I drove on, until, after
nearly two days' journey, my enemy was less than a mile away.

Now, just as he was within my grasp, the sea swelled
beneath the ice. The wind shrieked. The sea roared. And with
the mighty shock of an earthquake, the ice below me cracked
with the boom of thunder.

A raging sea rolled between me and my enemy, the gap between us widening. I was left drifting on a scattered piece of ice that shrank with every passing minute.

Hours passed. Several of my dogs died. Hope died. Cold and exhaustion overwhelmed me. I gave myself up to a terrible death and the misery of failure.

Then I saw your ship anchored and hope rose again. I quickly destroyed part of my sledge to make oars, and paddled myself closer.

The rest you know, Captain Walton.

Yet my task is unfinished – destruction of the demon. If I die, Captain Walton, swear to me that the monster won't escape, that you'll seek him out ...

Chapter 9

For a week I'd listened to Frankenstein's horrifying tale.
Telling it had weakened him. Daily his health worsened,
as the mountains of ice surrounded my ship and threatened
every moment to crush us. He could no longer leave his bed,
becoming weaker and weaker.

"You see where imagination and ambition have brought
me," he said. "I'm chained to an everlasting punishment.
I succeeded in the task of creating a new life. But I lacked
the wisdom to see what this would bring. In a fit of
enthusiastic madness I created him, a creature with feelings
and ideas. I should have given him, as far as was in my power,
his happiness ... "

Not long after that he could no
longer speak. I watched over him,
until he died.

Some time later, the night
calmed, and the winds lessened,
and I thought I heard a
strange, hoarse, inhuman voice
coming from the cabin where
Frankenstein's body lay in its coffin.

I rushed there. To my amazement a huge figure leant over the body. Long ragged locks of hair hid his face. He was weeping. One giant hand stretched out, as if pleading, its colour like the skin of the dead.

When he heard me enter, he sprang towards the window. I saw his face, repulsive, hideous. I called for him to stay. He paused and looked at me with wonder. He turned to Frankenstein's lifeless form again, and at once seemed to forget me.

"There, too, is my victim!" he cried. "With his death the miserable journey of my life closes. Oh Frankenstein, forgive me, for destroying you by destroying what you loved. Oh, he's cold! He can't answer! Once I hoped to be friends with excellent beings who would forgive my outward looks and love me for my good nature. I wanted honour and love from humans. Yet I had only loneliness and suffering. Now, no misery is greater than mine. He lies there, white and cold, my creator – the only one I could hope to be my friend."

He turned to me. "The hate you feel for me will be no greater than the hate I feel for myself. Know that I'll leave your ship and go to the most northern limits of the world, there to die. It's all that's left for me, for only bitter regret will poison me until death."

He looked at the body for a moment. "Farewell, Frankenstein," he said finally.

With that, he sprang from the cabin window, onto the ice-
raft that lay close to the ship.

And so ends my tale, too, as the story of Frankenstein
and his creature ends.

I watched him swept away by the waves, to be lost in
endless darkness and distance.

Making a monster

In an instant I knew without question that it was dangerous. It was too hideous to belong to the human race, and must be evil.

Ideas for reading

Written by Clare Dowdall, PhD

Lecturer and Primary Literacy Consultant

Reading objectives:
- identify and discuss themes and conventions in and across a wide range of writing
- making comparisons within and across books
- draw inferences such as inferring characters' feelings, thoughts and motives from their actions, and justifying inferences with evidence
- summarise the main ideas drawn from more than one paragraph, identifying key details that support the main ideas

Spoken language objectives:
- participate in discussions, presentations, performances, role play, improvisations and debates

Curriculum Links: Art and design – developing the imagination

Resources: Mask making materials; ICT

Build a context for reading

- Hand out the book and read the title. Ask children what they know about Frankenstein.
- Read the blurb and discuss what it says. Establish that Frankenstein is a doctor and not the monster shown in the illustration.
- Challenge children to think about the questions in the blurb. Do they think that life's events can shape our behaviour and personality, or are we born to behave in certain ways?

Understand and apply reading strategies

- Read the opening of the story together. Ask children to discuss who's talking to the reader. Explain that this type of story telling is a first person narrative.
- As a group, read to p9 and look at the text: "I began to tell him of our goal to explore unknown regions, to find undiscovered lands, to know more about Earth than ever imagined..." Discuss the narrator's goal and what this tells the reader about his character.